Until Proven Guilty

by

Nigel Hinton

First published in 2006 in Great Britain by
Barrington Stoke Ltd
18 Walker St, Edinburgh EH3 7LP

www.barringtonstoke.co.uk

Reprinted 2007

ISBN: 978-1-84299-369-9

Printed in Great Britain by Bell & Bain Ltd

To my nephew Chris Austin
– a computer wizard

Thanks for the website:
www.nigelhinton.net

Contents

A Note from the Author

I went to a very strict school and sometimes my friends and I got punished for things we hadn't done. Back then, when I read about murderers being put to death, I thought that maybe some of them were innocent, too. And, in fact, sometimes people *were* hanged for crimes they didn't commit.

Another thing I've often thought about is that whenever a serial killer is caught, no one ever says, "Yes, I always suspected he was a murderer." Instead the family and friends are shocked to find out that the person they love is a killer. People can hide the darkest secrets inside themselves and even their families don't know the truth.

Guilty or Innocent?

Chapter 1

The Phone Call

What a difference a day makes.

In less than 24 hours Nathan's life fell to bits. And it all started so well, with the phone call from Dad.

****

The phone rang during breakfast and Grace got to it before Nathan. She picked it up.

"Daddy!" Grace said. Nathan had to smile at his little sister. Dad was asking her questions and she was nodding and shaking her head as if Dad could see her. At last she said, "Bye, Daddy," and handed the phone to Nathan.

"Hi, Dad," Nathan said. He felt a big grin of happiness spread across his face. "How's Germany?"

"No, I'm home – just driven off the ferry. I got the delivery done fast so I thought I might grab a couple of hours' fishing before I take the truck back to the depot. You're on half-term, aren't you?"

"Yes," Nathan said.

"Well, bring the rods and I'll meet you down the bridge at three."

"Cool."

After breakfast Grace watched cartoons on TV and Nathan went online and played *Soccer Manager* until Auntie Jane came. She wasn't their real auntie but that's what she made them call her. She lived down the road and dropped in every day for a couple of hours in the holidays. She was a terrible gossip and Nathan didn't like her.

He'd told Mum a few times that he'd rather look after himself but she'd said, "I know, love. But Grace is only six and I feel happier if there's an adult to keep an eye on her. Besides it stops Jane getting lonely. The poor old dear's all on her own since her sister died."

As soon as Auntie Jane arrived, she made herself at home in the front room. She changed the TV channel to a chat programme so Grace got bored and asked Nathan to play with her. They went up to her room and he pretended to be interested while she played with her dolls.

"Oooh, fancy a boy your age playing with dolls," Auntie Jane said when she came upstairs later.

Nathan ignored her and Grace ran down to watch TV again.

"Did you hear about that crash on the motorway yesterday?" Auntie Jane asked. "It must be a worry for you – your father out on the roads in his lorry."

Nathan gave her an angry look and got up to go to his room. Auntie Jane followed him along the corridor to his room and stood in the doorway gossiping while he played computer games. She went on and on, saying horrible things about people who lived down the road, so he put the sound up loud so he couldn't hear her voice any more. At last she went off to watch another TV programme.

Grace came back upstairs and said she was hungry.

"What do you want?" Nathan asked.

"Beans on toast."

Nathan liked cooking. He wished his little sister would let him make something else but she always wanted beans on toast.

They were just finishing eating when Auntie Jane came in and said that she was going home.

"Beans again?" she said, looking at their plates. "Is that all you can cook?"

"'Bye, Auntie Jane," Nathan said, walking to the front door with her. "Thanks for coming round –"

Then he closed the door behind her and added, "– Not!"

Mum got back at 1.30 and Nathan made her a sandwich. Grace climbed onto her knee and cuddled her while she told them about her morning at the hospital where she worked as a receptionist.

"Mmmn, you do a great sandwich," Mum said and licked her fingers. "You're my favourite chef!"

Nathan looked at his watch. "Oh Mum, I've got to go. Dad rang. He's back and I'm meeting him at the river at three."

"Haven't you got football training?" she asked.

"Not until six. I'll take my kit and go straight there after fishing."

He got his things together and fetched his bike. "See you later," he called.

"OK. And tell your dad I'm sulking because he prefers fishing to me!" his mum laughed.

Nathan left the house and headed out of town towards the river.

It seemed like a normal afternoon. But during the next few days he would go over and over everything, trying to remember, and trying to make sense of it all.

Chapter 2

A Death

Afterwards, people asked Nathan what time he got to the bridge and he knew exactly. He always tried to beat his best time when he cycled from the house to the river. That afternoon he was really fast. When he checked his watch he saw that he'd taken less than half an hour. It was 2.28.

He sat on the bridge wall to get his breath back then walked slowly down to the river bank. He waited there, trying to spot some fish in the muddy water, until 2.45. His dad still wasn't due for a quarter of an hour but

Nathan felt a little jab of panic in his heart. It was Auntie Jane's fault – all that talk about crashes on the motorway. He began to worry. What if Dad had a crash?

As the minutes ticked by, he became more and more worried.

Three o'clock.

3.10.

3.20.

At 3.25 he walked back up to the bridge and looked along the road. No sign of his dad's lorry. He could feel his heart thumping.

He tried to tell himself that Dad might be stuck in traffic. But he still couldn't stop worrying. What would he do if Dad was killed in a crash? It would be terrible. Some of his mates didn't get on with their fathers but Dad was different. He was a laugh and easy to talk to. They were like real friends.

He checked his watch at 3.30, and again a few minutes later. Cars and trucks roared past, but still no sign of Dad.

At 3.40 he made up his mind to go home. He was pushing the bike back up the slope to the road when he saw Dad's lorry crossing the bridge. He dropped the bike and ran along to the lay-by.

"You're late!" he said as Dad climbed out of the cab.

There was a smile on Dad's face but his eyes flicked away from Nathan as he said, "Sorry, mate – you should have seen the traffic on the motorway."

They walked down to the river and along the bank to their favourite fishing spot.

As Nathan handed Dad the tackle box, he noticed the long scratch on the back of his hand.

"How did you do that?" he asked.

"It's nothing," Dad said.

"It's bleeding."

Dad grabbed the tackle box and turned away. "I'm going to try a bit further along the bank today. You can stay here."

He walked along the bank and sat down 20 metres away. A few minutes later Nathan saw him take a tissue from his pocket and wipe the scratch.

Nathan tried to concentrate on fishing but he kept looking over at his dad. He had his line in the water but he wasn't even watching the float. He was staring away across the river, lost in his thoughts.

It didn't feel right. Normally they had such a good time when they went fishing. They always stood side by side and chatted and had a laugh. But not today.

And when Dad got back from a trip he always had loads of stories to tell. But not today. Today it all felt different.

The fishing wasn't much fun either – not a single bite for nearly an hour. Then Nathan caught a fish but it was only small, so he took it off the hook and slipped it back into the river.

As he turned round to get some new bait he saw something move in the long grass near the hedge. He walked over for a closer look then turned away in horror. It was a dog, covered in blood. Flies were buzzing round it.

"Dad! Quick!" he called.

Dad dropped his rod and ran up to him. He bent down and looked at the dog.

"Been hit by a car," Dad said. "He's crawled down here to die."

"We'd better call a vet," Nathan said, turning away. He didn't want to look at that bloody shape in the grass.

"Too late for that. His jaw's broken off and his guts are half out," Dad said. "Looks as if his hip's broken, too – and his back legs. He'll be dead before the vet gets here. Better put him out of his agony."

"Kill him?"

"We can't let him suffer like this, Nath – it's cruel. Go over there if you don't want to watch."

Nathan moved away and looked at the river slowly flowing past.

He heard the dog growl, then his dad talking softly. There was a little whimper then a crack.

The hair stood up on the back of Nathan's neck.

"Poor thing's out of its misery now," his dad said, walking past him with the dead dog in his arms. He bent down and slid the dog's body into the river. It floated away on the muddy water. Then, slowly, it rolled over and sank.

"What did you do?" Nathan asked as he watched his dad wash the blood off his hands.

"Broke his neck. Quick and painless."

"God, Dad, how can you do it?"

"I've been in war zones, Nathan. When you've seen your pals shot or blown up or burned alive, you get used to death. Anyway, I was doing him a favour."

They both went back to fishing but Nathan's heart wasn't in it. He kept thinking about the dog, and at 5.15 he started to pack up his rod.

"Had enough?" Dad asked.

"Got training," he said.

"OK, I'll stay a bit longer. See you back at the house – I'll take your rod for you. 'Bye."

Nathan pushed his bike up the slope, then began pedalling along the road. He had just gone round the first bend when he heard the roar of an engine behind him. He looked over his shoulder and saw a white van speeding round the bend. It was going way too fast. It skidded onto the far side of the road then swerved back towards him. Nathan jerked the handlebars of his bike and threw himself onto the grassy bank as the van screamed past.

He stood up. There was dirt on his jeans and a graze on his hand. But he was lucky – if he hadn't got out of the way he would have been crushed like that poor dog.

He looked along the road.

"Stupid idiot!" he shouted but the van was already vanishing round another bend.

Chapter 3
The Training

Nathan slipped the ball past the defender and set off after it.

"Nath – here!" Nathan looked up and saw his friend, Ben Westcott, making a run towards the goal.

Nathan kicked the ball high into the centre and Ben met it with a perfect volley. The ball flew into the back of the net.

"Great goal," their coach called. "OK, lads – that'll do for today. Don't forget, there's another training on Friday."

17

"Crap pass, Nath," Ben joked as they walked towards the changing room with the others.

"Yeah, like your crap shot," Nathan laughed. He dodged away as Ben pretended to punch him.

But Ben didn't say much as they cycled home from the training ground and Nathan could see he was worried about something. They'd only been friends a little while – Ben's family had moved down from the north five months ago. But it felt as if they'd been best mates for years. They liked the same subjects at school, they liked the same video games, they both loved football, they had the same sense of humour and, on top of everything else, both their dads were drivers.

"Want to come in?" Nathan asked when they stopped outside his house.

Ben shook his head then looked at Nathan, "Hayley had to go back to hospital today for more chemo and the drugs they give her always make her feel sick."

So that's what Ben was upset about. His little sister had leukaemia and she had to keep going to hospital.

"Mum and Dad get stressed when Hayley's ill – especially Dad, so I'd better get home. See ya."

Nathan watched as his friend cycled away. Poor Ben.

As Nathan opened the front door he could hear his family upstairs. Dad was talking and Grace and Mum were roaring with laughter.

How lucky he was. Everything was OK.

Afterwards, he would look back at this moment – the last moment of total happiness.

Chapter 4
The Police Arrive

His mum was tired and went to bed at ten o'clock. Nathan and his dad flicked through the channels on the TV but they couldn't find anything good.

"Let's watch the DVD," his dad said and Nathan knew exactly which one he meant. 'Strait for Goal' – a film showing all the goals of their favourite player, Darren Strait. They'd watched it dozens of times but they never got fed up with it.

"This is my idea of a perfect evening," his dad said as the DVD started. "Sitting with you, watching old Darren. He's the best player I've ever seen."

"You always say that."

"That's 'cos it's true," his dad grinned.

They were about halfway through the film when there was a knock on the front door. His dad jumped in surprise then got up and peeked out of the window.

"It's the cops," he said softly. "Now what?"

He went out into the hall and a few seconds later he came back followed by two policemen.

"Go and make us some tea, will you, Nathan?"

Nathan went into the kitchen, put the kettle on and then tip-toed back to listen near the door.

"... a young woman called Lucy Holden?" one of the policeman was saying. "This is her photo."

"No, never seen her," his dad said. "What about her?"

"I'm afraid she's been found dead in Hamley Woods early this evening. Someone saw your lorry parked at the bridge not far from there."

"Yes, I was fishing with my son."

"Right. We wondered if you saw anything that might help us. Someone else around? Anything at all, really."

There was a long silence then his dad said, "Sorry – can't think of anything."

Nathan heard the kettle boiling and he dashed into the kitchen and made the tea. He put the mugs onto a tray and carried them to the sitting room. His hands trembled as he handed them round.

"Your dad tells us you went fishing this afternoon," one of the policemen said. "Do you remember what time you got there?"

"Twenty-eight minutes past two."

"Wow, that's precise," the policeman said with a smile. "And your dad arrived at ...?"

"Twenty to four – I checked my watch because ..." Nathan stopped because the policeman suddenly turned to his dad.

"I thought you said you got there at three o'clock," the policeman said.

"No, no – I was meant to be there at three but I got held up in traffic," his dad said.

The policeman wrote in his notebook then turned back to Nathan. "Did you see anyone else around near the river or on the bridge while you were waiting for your dad? Anything odd?"

Nathan shook his head.

The policeman asked a few more questions then he closed his notebook. He looked at Dad for a long moment before standing up.

"Right, we'll be getting along," he said. "Sorry to disturb you. And if you remember anything that might help us, just give us a call."

Nathan waited while his dad showed the policemen out.

"Time for bed," his dad said when he came back.

"But what about ...?" Nathan began. He was dying to talk about it all.

"I said bed!" his dad cut in. His voice was sharp and angry, so Nathan didn't argue.

He went to bed. Why was Dad angry with him? He lay there for ages, listening for him to come upstairs, but in the end, he drifted off to sleep.

Nathan woke a couple of hours later. The light was still on in the corridor so he got out of bed and crept downstairs.

His dad was sitting on the sofa, his head in his hands.

"Are you angry with me?" Nathan asked.

"No, of course not," Dad said, looking up. He shook his head then added, "I'm angry with myself."

"Why?"

"Because I've done something stupid. Really stupid."

"What?"

His dad took a deep breath. "I lied to the cops. I told them I didn't see that girl, but I did. I gave her a lift. She was by the side of the road when I came off the motorway and I ... picked her up. I dropped her near Hamley Woods. And now she's dead."

"Why didn't you tell them?"

"I don't know. I don't know. Panic or something." His dad stopped, then looked right at Nathan. "You know what the cops are going to think, don't you?"

There was nothing to say. Nathan just sat there, his heart thudding and his face burning.

"Better go to bed, mate," his dad said at last, trying to smile. "Go on. I'll sort it tomorrow. It'll be OK, honest."

Nathan lay in bed. But he couldn't sleep. His mind raced over what Dad had said. Over and over, until the black night turned into grey morning.

Chapter 5
Questions

Nathan was already dressed when he heard Mum get up but he stayed in his room – Dad would need time to explain things to her. But half an hour later Grace got up so he went downstairs with her.

He saw Mum quickly wipe her eyes as they came into the room. She started chatting to Grace as if nothing was wrong. Dad pretended that he needed Nathan's help in the garage and when they got out there, he closed the door and spoke in a low voice.

"I've talked it over with Mum and she thinks I should explain things to the cops. So I'll drop in at the depot to ask for some time off, then I'll go down the police station. We don't want Grace to know anything about this – OK?"

It was hard trying to act normal with Grace when his mind was full of worries about Dad. And it was even harder when Auntie Jane arrived.

"Ooh, I heard you had a visit from the police last night," she said as soon as she got through the front door.

"What police?" Grace asked.

"It was nothing," he said to Grace. He gave Auntie Jane an angry look. "They just wanted to ask Dad something about lorries. Hey, your cartoon's on."

Grace ran in to watch the TV and Nathan walked into the kitchen.

29

"I thought it might be about that girl they found dead in Hamley Woods," Auntie Jane said, following him. "It was on the local news this morning. Lucy Holden. Only nineteen, she was."

"I didn't hear it," Nathan said coldly. "And you'd better not talk about stuff like that in front of Grace, you'll scare her."

He stayed with Grace all morning to make sure that Auntie Jane didn't bring the subject up and he was glad when Mum came home and Auntie Jane left. But he didn't stay glad for long. Mum closed the kitchen door.

"I don't want Grace to know about this," she said. She bit her lip to stop herself from crying, then went on.

"I've got some bad news. Dad called me at work. When he got to the depot the police were searching his truck. They found the girl's fingerprints in his cab so they knew he'd lied to them. They've taken him to the police station and they've been questioning him all morning. He's asked me to find a lawyer."

And now the tears spilled down her cheeks.

Nathan felt helpless. He didn't know what to do. Then Mum suddenly wiped the tears away with her hands and stood taller.

"No crying," she said, almost to herself. Then she looked at Nathan and added, "We've got to be strong and help Dad. You take care of Grace while I go into town."

Mum didn't get home until early evening. And it was only when Grace was in bed that she told Nathan what had happened. She'd found a lawyer called Mr Baxter and they'd gone to the police station together.

"They wouldn't let me in but Mr Baxter was with Dad for two hours. They're still questioning him and Mr Baxter thinks they won't release him until tomorrow at the earliest."

"But they are going to let him go?" Nathan asked. "Right? Mum? They are, aren't they?" He needed her to say yes. He needed some hope to stop this terrible pain that was squeezing his heart. But she just shook her head. She didn't know. And he realised that she was as scared and lost as he was. She reached over and gripped his hand tight and they sat there, side by side. Not saying anything. Just holding each other's hands.

Chapter 6

The Long Dark Hours

Nathan had another bad night. He kept telling himself that it would be OK, kept telling himself that Dad would be released in the morning. But, as the long dark hours crawled by, he couldn't stop his brain racing. Maybe the police would make a mistake. Sometimes innocent men were found guilty. Maybe Dad would be sent to prison.

And then, the worst thought of all – maybe he had done it.

It was a stupid, terrible thought. But he couldn't make it go away. Why had Dad lied to the police? And why had he turned up late at the river? And there'd been something weird about him – almost like he was acting guilty. And the way he'd just coolly broken that dog's neck and said you got used to death when you'd seen your mates die. Maybe he hadn't dropped the girl near Hamley Woods. Maybe he'd killed her.

No, no – his dad couldn't be a murderer. Not his dad. He couldn't be.

Could he?

Nathan was tired next morning and the last person he wanted to see was Auntie Jane. She didn't say anything at first, just watched the TV. But when Grace went next door to play with her friend Lily she came up to Nathan's room.

"Seems I was right, then," Auntie Jane said, standing in the doorway.

He went on playing his computer game, hoping she would go away.

"My friend's cousin is a policeman. He says they've got your dad down at the station. Asking him questions."

He still didn't turn round but he could feel his anger rising.

"About that dead girl," she added.

"Shut up," he said softly.

"Must be a worry for you. You know what they say – no smoke without fire."

And now the anger broke. He got up. Four steps and he was face to face with her. He saw a look of shock in her eyes.

"Get out!" he said.

"I was only telling you what ..."

"Get out or I'll throw you out!"

He meant it and she knew it. She turned away and started down the stairs. He followed her then ran to the door and opened it wide. She walked out, not looking back at him. He waited until she reached the garden gate then he slammed the door.

He sat on the stairs and felt good – he had done the right thing. But when his mum got home she told him that he'd made a big mistake.

"You know what Jane's like," Mum said. "I expect she's told the whole street by now."

And his mum was right. About ten minutes later Grace came home in tears.

"Lily ... says ... Daddy ... is a ... b-bad man," Grace sobbed. "She says he'll have to go to prison."

Mum made up her mind there and then. "I'm taking Grace to stay with Nan until all this blows over," she told Nathan. "Do you want to go with her?"

He thought how good it would be to be out in the country, 40 miles away from Auntie Jane and all the other whispering gossips. But he shook his head and told Mum the truth. "I want to be with you."

Chapter 7
Murder. Murder. Murder.

Mum didn't get back from Nan's house until the evening. Nathan was just making some tea for her when someone knocked on the door. A tall, very thin man with white hair was standing there. His blue eyes peered at Nathan.

"You look very much like your father," he said. "I'm his lawyer, Joshua Baxter."

Nathan led Mr Baxter into the kitchen and he shook hands with Mum.

"I'm afraid I've got some bad news," he said. "Your husband has been charged with the murder of Lucy Holden."

Nathan saw his mum gripping the top of the chair, to stop herself from falling.

"You said they'd let him go today," she whispered.

"That's what I hoped, but the situation has changed. They found some of his skin under Miss Holden's fingernails. They think she scratched him as she struggled to get free."

The scratch on his dad's hand. Nathan remembered how his dad had grabbed the tackle box and walked away from him. It was as if he'd wanted to hide the scratch. As if he was guilty.

"There's something else," Mr Baxter went on. "The police are trying to link him with two other murders near Newcastle last year. Girls about the same age. Both killed the same way. They checked the records at the depot and they found out that he was delivering to a factory not far from Newcastle when the first girl was murdered. On the day of the second murder he was in Sheffield, over a hundred miles south of there. I pointed that out to the police. The problem is, that evening he clocked in late. So the police say he had time to drive up to Newcastle and back."

There was something Nathan had to know. Something he had to ask. But he was scared of what the answer might be.

"How were the girls killed?" he asked.

Mr Baxter turned his pale blue eyes to Nathan.

"Their necks were broken," he said.

Nathan could feel the blood throbbing in his throat. He sat down at the table and stared at the cup in front of him. He had put the milk in but he hadn't poured the tea. He stared at it, too numb to do anything, too numb to listen while his mum and Mr Baxter went on talking. Their necks were broken – like that dog.

How often had Nathan heard people on TV saying they couldn't believe that the nice person from next door had turned out to be a murderer or a terrorist. Human beings could hide dark and terrible secrets in their hearts. Was it really possible that Dad – the man he loved and trusted – had killed three girls?

He sat there, not moving, until Mr Baxter tapped him on the shoulder.

"I'd like you to do something for me," the lawyer said. "I want you to try to remember everything you can about that afternoon. I'll drop by tomorrow morning and see if you've thought of anything useful. Will you do that?"

Nathan nodded. As if he had a choice. As if he would be able to stop his brain from going over and over the same thing all night. The river. The death. His dad.

Chapter 8
Trying to Remember

By the time Mr Baxter arrived the next morning, Nathan was sure that Dad was guilty. The more he thought about it, the more it all fitted together – his dad being late, the scratch, the weird way he'd behaved, the way he'd killed the dog. So what should he do? Tell the lawyer everything and make Dad's case look worse? Or should he hide the truth from him? Lie to him?

In the end he didn't have to hide or lie. Mr Baxter didn't want to know anything about Dad. Instead he kept asking if Nathan could remember seeing anything odd on the river bank or on the bridge. Nathan told him about the dog and what Dad had done. But he said his dad had "put the dog out of his misery" rather than "killed him".

"Nothing else?" Mr Baxter asked again. "No people behaving strangely? Nothing unusual about the cars going past?" the lawyer asked.

Nathan shook his head. Then he suddenly remembered something. "There was a white van," he said. "It was going really fast. It nearly knocked me off my bike."

Mr Baxter looked up, interested. "What else? Can you remember anything more? Any details?" But all Nathan could say was that the van had been white and going too fast.

Then Mr Baxter made him close his eyes. He told him to relax and breathe deeply then he began talking to him softly, trying to take Nathan back to that moment. He asked him to picture himself leaving his dad. He asked him to picture himself walking up the bank to the bridge, getting on the bike. And then what?

Nathan could see it and he described it to Mr Baxter. Cycling along the road, going round the bend. Then the screeching tyres. Looking back, seeing the van swerve across the road towards him.

"The driver. Can you see the driver?" Mr Baxter asked.

"No, the sun was shining on the windscreen – it was just a flash of light."

"What about the van? Any marks? Any writing on it?"

Nathan squeezed his eyes shut, trying to see, trying to remember.

"I think there was something blue on the back ... a kind of sign or something, but it all happened so fast ..."

And he couldn't remember anything else, no matter how hard he tried. No matter how many times Mr Baxter talked him through it.

"Well, I'll tell the police, but it doesn't give them much to go on," the lawyer said as he was leaving. "If you think of anything else, you must tell me at once. If we could find that driver, he might have seen something that could help us."

Nathan felt better – maybe his dad hadn't killed that girl. Maybe that driver would be able to prove it. He decided to go back to the river to see if that would make him remember something else about the van. As he cycled past Auntie Jane's house, he could see her standing at the front window – watching the street as usual, checking what everyone was up to. He felt like giving her a rude sign but she ducked back behind the curtain.

He turned the corner to the row of shops and skidded to a halt. Outside the newsagents there was a board for the local newspaper. There was a headline written on it: DEAD GIRL – LOCAL MAN ARRESTED.

Nathan stood there and stared at the words. 'Local Man'. Dad's name would be in the paper. People all over town would read about him and think he was a murderer. There were two women outside the shop. They looked over at Nathan and started talking. And he knew what they were saying – "There he is. That's the murderer's son!"

He turned round and pedalled home as fast as he could. He ran indoors and closed the curtains. He sat on the sofa until his mum came home. She had a copy of the paper. She showed him the huge headline then ripped the paper in half and threw it onto a chair.

At that moment the phone rang.

"It's probably Nan," she said and went to pick it up. "Hello?"

Nathan was looking at her and saw her face change. She didn't say a word, just listened. Then she clicked the phone off and stood with it in her hand.

"Who was it, Mum?"

"I don't know," she said, shaking her head. "Some bloke ... some sick bloke saying terrible things about Dad. Oh God, Nathan, what are we going to do?"

For the rest of the afternoon, they held on to each other. The phone kept ringing but they didn't answer it. They just stayed there. Not crying. Not talking. Just hiding from the world in the half-dark room.

Chapter 9

Trapped

During the next week Nathan felt like a trapped animal in a cage.

Mum decided to take time off work. She rang Nathan's school and told them he'd be away for a while after half-term.

They unplugged the phone to stop the endless hate calls. And when the hate letters started coming, they stopped opening their post, too. They kept the curtains closed and the doors locked.

One night someone threw a brick through one of their windows. The next morning they had to board it up. And the next night someone started a fire against their front door. They managed to put it out with a bucket of water but now they were scared. They decided to sleep downstairs so that they could escape if there was a real blaze.

One day there was a knock at the door and Nathan opened it to find two newspaper reporters there. They started asking questions but he tried to close the door.

"We're giving you the chance to put your side of the story," one of them said, and put his foot against the door to block it open.

"We've got nothing to say," Nathan said.

"What's your dad like? Does he go away a lot?"

"Nothing to say."

"Look, give us an interview or we'll print what people are saying about him."

"Go away!" Nathan shouted.

"We heard he's got a bit of drink problem and he knocks your mum about. You don't want that in the papers, do you?"

There was a flash, as one of them took a photo and then Nathan felt his mum by his side. They both pushed with all their strength and closed the door.

For the next few days they didn't open the door to anyone. It was him and his mum against the world. They didn't watch TV or listen to the radio in case there was something about Dad, and the only contact they had with the outside world was when Mum used Nathan's mobile to call Nan. She didn't even do that very often because it made her cry when she talked to Grace.

By the end of the week the letters had stopped coming. The word KILLER was still painted on the front wall, but the teenagers who had written it weren't hanging around on the pavement anymore. So, on the Saturday morning when someone knocked on the door, Nathan opened it.

It was Ben Westcott.

And Ben did everything right. He didn't ask questions and he didn't talk about the arrest or the newspaper. He just acted as if everything was normal. They went up to Nathan's room and played game after game of Space Kings on the computer and Ben told jokes and made him laugh for the first time in ages.

"Thanks for coming round," he said as Ben was leaving. "It was great to see you."

"Yeah, good to see you, too," Ben said. "I missed your ugly face at school. And it's been well grim at home, too. Hayley's been bad after all the chemo. Mum's really down about it and my old man's in a right state. Oh, he said he's sorry to hear about your dad."

Nathan shrugged but he was touched. It was really kind of Ben's dad. Not everyone was cruel and filled with hate. There were people who were nice and thought of others even when they had their own problems.

"Hey, you coming to the match tomorrow?" Ben asked. "You're down to play."

Nathan was going to say no. He didn't feel like seeing people yet but Ben grabbed his arm. "Come on," he said, "it'll cheer us both up. I'll be able to laugh at your crap crosses!"

"Yeah, for your crap shots! OK then."

As Nathan stood and watched Ben walk away, Mr Baxter drew up in his car.

For a short time he had been able to forget his troubles, but now they all came rushing back as Mr Baxter started talking to him and his mum about the police and the murder of the three girls. Nathan sat there and listened. Everything Mr Baxter said pointed to Dad's guilt. He felt more and more miserable. When Mr Baxter said that Dad had sent his love and was missing them, Nathan couldn't stop himself–

"Well, he should have thought about that before he went and ruined everything."

"Nathan!" his mum said in a shocked voice.

He got up and ran upstairs. He felt angry and ashamed and mixed up as he sat on his bed. About ten minutes later Mr Baxter knocked on his door and came in. His blue eyes looked straight at him and Nathan turned away and stared at the floor.

"Why do you think your father is guilty?" Mr Baxter asked.

Nathan shrugged his shoulders. "Well, the police do, don't they," he mumbled, still looking at the floor.

"I'm not interested in the police, I'm interested in you. Come on, tell me."

So Nathan told him, "He lied to me. He said he was held up in traffic but he was with that girl. And he was acting all weird – like he was hiding something."

There was a long silence and Nathan looked up and saw Mr Baxter's eyes fixed on him.

"How old are you?" Mr Baxter asked.

"Fourteen."

"Old enough to understand things, then. Shall I tell you why your father seemed weird? Because he was embarrassed."

"Why?"

"Because when he picked up that girl he thought she was just a hitchhiker. But she wasn't. She only pretended she needed a lift so that drivers would stop for her. All she wanted was money. And she would do anything to get it. Anything." Mr Baxter looked at Nathan. "You understand?"

Nathan nodded, then Mr Baxter went on. "She asked your father to drop her at that lonely car park in Hamley woods. But when they got there, she offered to have sex with him. He said he wasn't interested and told her to get out. Then, as she was climbing out of the cab, she tried to steal his wallet from the bag which was on the floor. He grabbed the wallet back and that's when she scratched his hand. She said that if he didn't give her some money she'd tell the police he'd tried to rape her. He ignored her and made her get out of the lorry. Then he drove off to meet you."

"Why didn't he tell me all that?" Nathan asked.

"Come on, Nathan! He was shaken up. Plus he felt he'd been a fool to give her a lift in the first place. Of course he didn't want to talk to you about it."

"Did he tell you this?"

"Yes," Mr Baxter said.

"And you believe him?"

"Of course, I believe him," Mr Baxter said, "And you should, too. You know him. You know what a good, honest man he is. I'd stake my life on it – your father is innocent. And somehow I've got to prove it to the rest of the world."

Chapter 10

Memories

Nathan woke early again the next morning. It was still dark. But instead of feeling lost and hopeless like he had done all week, he was full of positive thoughts. He lay there thinking about his dad. He could hear Mr Baxter's words – "You know what a good, honest man he is."

Yes, he was. And a great dad.

Nathan let all the happy memories come flooding back.

How excited he used to get when he was a little kid and he knew Dad was coming home on leave from the army. The excitement would build and build for days until that magic moment when Dad walked through the door and lifted you up to hug you. That was Dad. He was either holding you in his arms, or he was down on the floor, playing with you at your level. Always face to face. And Nathan could see that face now – the smiling eyes, the shiny hair, the stubble that was fun to stroke but which prickled every time Dad kissed you or gave you a cuddle.

Then Nathan remembered how sad he felt when Dad had to go away again. How he missed him. When he started school and did his first squiggly drawings and paintings, his teacher would ask what he had drawn and he would always say, "My daddy in the army."

How happy he was when Dad had left the army just after Grace was born. His job as a truck-driver meant that he was still away a lot, but never for so long. There was much more time for playing together and talking together and being together. The games of cricket in the garden. Kicking the football about in the park. His dad teaching him to fish. His dad taking him to football games. Watching matches on TV together. Both of them playing with Grace and taking her for walks. And the silly jokes. And his dad acting stupid and making him laugh about nothing.

And how proud he'd been when they were out in town one day and met one of Dad's old mates from the army. The man had bent down to Nathan and said, "Know what? Your dad saved my life. He pulled me out of my tank just before it exploded. I bet he didn't tell you that, did he? But he's the bravest bloke I've ever met."

How could he have forgotten all that? How could he ever have thought that Dad had killed those girls?

Well, he wouldn't forget again. From now on he would believe in his dad and he'd do everything he could to stand up for him and to help him.

Chapter 11
Fighting Mad

Nathan didn't have long to wait before he stood up for his dad.

He turned up for the football match and everything seemed to be great. All his team mates welcomed him and none of them said anything about what had happened.

As they were getting changed, the coach told Ben that a couple of professional scouts were coming to the game to watch him. Nathan was really pleased for his friend, but Ben took it all calmly.

"Yeah, I know what they're like," he said. "I had about five of them come and see me when I was playing for Tyne Juniors, where we lived before. There was even one guy from United. They watch you for about ten minutes then they shoot off to watch some other kid in some other game and you never hear anything."

"You never know," Nathan said. "They might see you score one of your crap goals and sign you up for a load of money."

"Well, you'd better make sure you send over plenty of your crap crosses then," Ben laughed.

The game started well. Nathan made some good runs down the wing. He managed to skip past the defender who was marking him, and cross the ball to Ben. Then, as he set off on another run, the defender threw himself into a tackle and knocked Nathan off his feet.

The referee blew for a foul and booked the defender.

As the players got ready for the free kick, the defender walked past Nathan. "Next time, I'll break your neck – like your dad did to that girl," he snarled.

For a moment Nathan was too shocked to do anything. Then he set off after him. He grabbed hold of him, swung him round, and punched him full in the face. The defender fell to the ground, blood pouring from his nose. The next second there were people all over Nathan, pushing and shoving him. He punched out at them but then he was dragged back by someone. It was Ben.

"Leave off, mate! Leave off!" his friend was shouting.

But it was too late. The referee produced a red card and Nathan was sent off.

"What the hell's the matter with you?" his coach asked, but Nathan walked straight past him to the changing rooms.

He didn't even wait for the end of the game. He got changed and went home.

Ben kept texting him on his mobile but Nathan didn't reply. He knew he'd been wrong to punch the guy. And on top of that, he might have messed up his best friend's chance of getting noticed by the football scouts. He felt ashamed and he promised himself that he wouldn't let it happen again.

He broke the promise the very next day when he went back to school.

At lunch time he was talking to Ben near the drinks machine. A couple of boys from Year 11 were mucking about and one of them banged into Nathan and spilt his drink.

"Hey, watch it!" Nathan said.

"Yeah, you'd better watch it," the other Year 11 boy said to his friend, "or he'll murder you!"

A wild burst of anger shot through Nathan and he pushed the boy hard and knocked him to the ground. Ben tried to drag him away, but he broke free and charged. The boy was much bigger than him but Nathan was crazy with rage. He jumped on him and punched him hard.

The next moment he felt himself pulled upwards by a teacher. He was pushed back against the wall. The other boy got to his feet, blood running from a cut on his lip.

The two of them were marched to the Head Teacher's office. The Head was furious and she called his mum and told her that Nathan was excluded for a week.

"I don't care what the boy did, I'm ashamed of you," his mum said when she'd heard what had happened. "And if you think going round fighting people is helping your dad, you'd better think again."

She was right – fighting wouldn't help Dad. But Nathan had thought of something that would. He was going to use the week off school to look for the driver of that white van.

Chapter 12
The Hunt

"What do you do all day, laze in bed?" Ben asked when he dropped in after school to see Nathan.

"Cycle round town," said Nathan.

"What for?"

"Dunno," he said. He suddenly felt that he couldn't explain, even to Ben. *What was he doing? And why?* Looking for a white van! Even if he saw it – what would he do? Would he talk to the driver? Why would the driver even remember that afternoon? It really did seem like a waste of time.

But Nathan couldn't just give up. He clung to the hope that maybe the driver had seen something. Something that would help to free Dad.

"How's school?" Nathan asked.

"Same as ever," Ben replied. "Better than home, though."

"Why?"

"Hayley's ill. The doctor thinks the chemo's working but the poor kid's sick all the time and she's losing her hair. It'll grow back but she's well upset. And that upsets Mum. My dad's the worst, though. He's, like, totally depressed – doesn't talk, doesn't eat. He was a bit like that when Hayley first got ill last summer but it's worse this time. Makes the whole house miserable."

"Better to have your dad there than not," Nathan said. Ben nodded and gave him a friendly pat on his shoulder.

The next day Nathan spent hour after hour going round town looking for the white van. Then he called at his friend's house on the way home. Mr and Mrs Westcott were both out at work so Ben was looking after Hayley. The little girl was pale and thin. Her long hair was almost all gone so she had a pink baseball cap on. The word Princess was written on the front. Ben was sweet to her, trying to cheer her up by mucking about. Nathan joined in and was pleased when the stupid things they did made her giggle.

As he was leaving he saw Mr Westcott slowly walking up the road. His head was bent down, as if his troubles were too heavy for him.

"Hi, Mr Westcott," Nathan called out as he cycled by.

Mr Westcott glanced at him then looked away. Nathan was surprised and hurt but, when he thought about it, he understood. Mr Westcott was so sad about Hayley that he couldn't even face having to talk to people. Nathan knew that feeling. It was what he'd felt when he and his mum had hidden away from the world.

All week Nathan hunted for the white van. A couple of times his heart flipped when he thought he'd spotted it but when he looked closer it wasn't the one. There seemed to be thousands of white vans. Would he even recognize it if he *did* see it again? After all, he couldn't remember much about it. Perhaps it had come from another part of the country and was hundreds of miles away. No, he didn't believe that. Deep in his heart he was sure it was somewhere in town and one day he would see it. And when he did, he would know it was the one.

Grace came home from Nan's that week-end, and on the Monday both of them went back to school. Life seemed almost normal again – Mum and him and Grace together. It was as if Dad was just away on one of his trips. Except he wasn't, he was in prison, charged with murder.

Mr Baxter came round on Tuesday evening and told them that Dad had been refused bail but that they could visit him in prison.

He also said that he'd been thinking about the second murder in Newcastle last summer. The police said that Dad had done his delivery in Sheffield, driven up to Newcastle, murdered the girl, then driven home. Mr Baxter had checked the timesheets at the depot and they showed that Dad had got back at nine o'clock that evening. That meant that even if Dad had driven at top speed he would only have had about 20 minutes to find the girl and kill her. It was almost impossible.

"But we need stronger evidence." Mr Baxter said. "The trouble is, the police think he did it. So they're not going to look any further. We need a break – something to change their minds."

Two days later they got their break.

Nathan saw the van in town.

Chapter 13

The Prisoner

Nathan was on the top deck of the school bus, talking to Ben. He looked down along a side street and saw a white van nosing its way out of a parking space. As the van came out from behind a car, his heart jumped in shock – there was a blue sign on the back. He couldn't see it clearly but he knew it was the one ...

The bus sped on and it didn't stop for another half a mile. Nathan knew there was nothing he could do. By the time he got back to the side street the van would be long gone.

But at least he knew that the driver was still in town. Now all he had to do was track him down.

That evening he cycled back to the street where he'd seen the van. What had the driver been doing here? Delivering something? Picking up something? Or had he stopped to grab a bite at that café over there?

He would keep a watch on this street – maybe the driver would come back. He stopped taking the bus to school and went by bike so that he'd be able to follow the van, if he ever spotted it again. Every morning and evening he hung around there but he saw nothing. He was planning to check the street at the weekend too, but something else came up. They had a letter from the prison to say they could visit Dad on the Saturday.

Nathan slept badly the night before the visit and he was shaking with nerves when he walked through the prison gates with his mum. They were shown into a large room with all the other visitors. Five minutes later the prisoners came in. Dad looked awful – thin and pale and dark eyed. Nathan had to fight back tears when he saw him.

They sat opposite him and the terrible hour crawled by. Mum and Dad tried to keep a conversation going. They kept on asking each other questions, but no one was in the mood for talking. All Nathan wanted to do was hold on to his dad and hug him but he couldn't do that here in this crowded, smelly room.

"You haven't said much," his dad said as the visit came to the end. "Are you OK, mate?"

Nathan nodded and then, before he could stop them, the tears filled his eyes and rolled down his face.

"Oh don't cry, Nath, don't cry," Dad said, his voice cracking with pain. "I didn't do it. Whatever it looks like, I didn't do it."

"I know," Nathan managed to say.

The next second his dad was led away with the other prisoners.

Chapter 14

The Hunt Pays Off

Although he kept looking, Nathan didn't see the van again for over two weeks. Then one evening he was cycling home from football training. It was nearly dark when he reached Westgate, the long hill that led out of town. Far below, at the bottom of the hill, he saw a white van come out of a side turning.

He sped down the slope and his eyes watered in the rush of cold air. He was going so fast that he nearly caught up with the van. He got closer and closer and now he could see the logo on the back – a blue D with two wavy lines going across it. He was so close he could even see the steering wheel and the driver's hands reflected in the side mirror. A bit closer and he might even see the driver's face.

He reached the end of the flat and started up the next hill. The bike began to slow. He pedalled hard but the van was drawing away from him. Further and further away up the slope. Nathan couldn't keep up. When he got to the top, a few minutes later, the van had gone.

He had lost it again. Perhaps it was gone forever. No, he'd seen the logo – the blue D and the two wavy lines. He could tell Mr Baxter and the police would be able to trace it.

As soon as he got home he rang Mr Baxter's office but his secretary said that he had gone away. He wouldn't be back until the day after tomorrow. Nathan asked if he had a mobile number, but she wouldn't give it to him.

Four hours later, as he was lying in bed thinking, he suddenly had an idea. The van had been heading out towards the industrial estate. Maybe that's where the van's depot was. Maybe the driver had been going there? If Nathan hung around at the same place tomorrow he might see it again.

And that's exactly what happened. Nathan waited on the main road near the estate and just before 5.30 he saw the van flash past. He set off after it. The van turned left at the traffic lights, then left again at the end of the road. It was going fast but Nathan managed to keep it in view until he saw it slow and turn in to a car park. Nathan cycled up to the turning and then stopped.

The van had parked against one of the buildings.

He saw the brake lights go off.

A moment later the van door slid open and the driver got out.

It was Ben's dad, Mr Westcott.

Chapter 15

A Scary Thought

What had stopped him from going up to Mr Westcott and talking to him? What had made him hide in the shadows as Mr Westcott walked out of the yard?

Nathan thought about it all evening and he didn't know. It had been such a shock to see Mr Westcott get out of that van. He'd always thought that Ben's dad drove big lorries, heavy goods trucks like Dad.

He went over and over it in his head. All his hopes had depended on finding the driver.

But he'd found the driver and it was no use. If Mr Westcott knew something that could prove Dad was innocent he would have gone to the police already. Wouldn't he?

Should he tell Mr Baxter that he'd found the driver anyway? No. What was the point?

Should he go round and see Mr Westcott? No, he couldn't do that. The poor bloke already had enough worries of his own. But maybe all his worries about Hayley had made him forget some important little detail about that day. If Nathan asked him some questions it might jog his memory.

Did Mr Westcott remember how he'd nearly knocked someone off a bike? Did he know that it had been Nathan? No, he couldn't know that. He would have stopped. Wouldn't he? Wouldn't he?

Even if he hadn't known it was Nathan on the bike, he must have known that he'd nearly had an accident. He should have stopped. And why had he been going so fast? That was the day Hayley had gone to hospital for her first chemo. Perhaps he'd been rushing back home to see her. That must be it.

Then, as Nathan was getting ready for bed, he thought of something else. Maybe it hadn't been Mr Westcott in the van. Maybe there was another van with the same logo. Maybe the company had dozens of vans. That would explain everything.

But when he woke up early the next morning Nathan knew there was something else that would explain everything. Something that he hadn't let himself think. Something that had been hidden deep down inside him ever since he saw Mr Westcott get out of the van last night.

What if Mr Westcott had killed that girl?

It was a scary thought. And Nathan knew now why he hadn't wanted to talk to Mr Westcott last night. He had been scared.

But Mr Westcott couldn't be a murderer. He just couldn't be.

Why not? That would explain why he'd been speeding. It would explain why he hadn't stopped. It would explain why he hadn't gone to the police.

And then Nathan remembered the other two girls. They had been murdered near Newcastle. Nathan knew that Ben and his family had lived up north, but he'd never asked where.

And there was something else – those two girls had been murdered last summer. Ben had said his dad had been depressed at that time because Hayley had got ill. But maybe it hadn't been Hayley's illness – maybe he had got depressed because he had been scared of being caught.

It still seemed impossible but it would be easy to clear up. All Nathan had to do was ask some questions.

But it was harder than he thought.

The next day at school he tried to find the right moment to ask Ben, but he felt awkward. Maybe Ben would see where the questions were leading. Maybe he would be hurt or angry. Then Nathan thought about Dad – pale and thin and alone in prison. If Mr Westcott had killed those girls and he was letting Dad take the blame ...

He felt a wave of anger sweep over him and the anger finally helped him to ask the question, "Are there are a lot of drivers where your dad works?"

"No, it's just a small company," Ben said, "so it's only him at the moment. But they're thinking of getting a couple more vans soon."

So – it was Mr Westcott in the van the day Lucy Holden was killed. Now for the big one.

"That club you used to play for, Tyne Juniors – where is it?"

"Swinley," Ben replied, "where we lived."

"Never heard of it," Nathan said.

"Oh, it's only a small place. It's about 20 miles outside Newcastle."

Chapter 16

Guilty

That afternoon Nathan rang Mr Baxter as soon as he got home from school. He told him everything.

"That's interesting," Mr Baxter said. But he didn't sound very excited. "I'll look into it."

Nathan put the phone down. And then suddenly he didn't feel sure about anything. After all, it didn't really add up to much. Mr Westcott had driven past Hamley Woods on the day of the murder. So what? Hundreds of people must have driven past that day. Mr Westcott had lived near Newcastle. So what? Thousands and thousands of people must live there. It didn't prove anything.

There was no news from Mr Baxter the next day. And no news the day after. Nathan began to think he'd made a bad mistake.

Then, the following day, Ben wasn't in school.

When Nathan got home, Mr Baxter was in the kitchen talking to Mum.

"They've taken that driver in for questioning," Mr Baxter said. "Things are looking up."

Mum went to bed early but Nathan stayed up to watch the football highlights on TV. So he was the only one awake when the phone rang at 10.45.

"Nathan?" It was Mr Baxter. "Good news – your father is being released tomorrow morning. That other driver's DNA matches up with some that they found on the victims. He's confessed and they're charging him with all three murders."

Chapter 17

No Monsters

What a difference a day makes.

Twenty-four hours ago Dad had been in prison. Twenty-four hours ago the whole world had thought he was the son of a murderer.

And now Dad was home and it was like a madhouse. The phone rang non-stop with calls from friends, and neighbours kept coming to the door to welcome him back.

"Where were they all a couple of weeks ago?" Mum asked in a sarcastic voice.

There was even a card from Auntie Jane on the door mat. She said how happy she was that things had worked out. Mum tore it up and put it in the dustbin.

Dad didn't care, though. He was like a kid, laughing and mucking around like crazy. He was bursting with energy and he couldn't sit still. He kept dancing around the room with Grace on his back. He kept kissing and cuddling Mum while she giggled and told him to stop being so daft. And he kept hugging Nathan.

"Do you know what stopped me going nuts when I was in prison?" he said. "Thinking of all the fishing I was going to do when I got out. And the footie I was going to play with you. And the bike rides. And the Darren Strait DVD. And now I can do all of them and I don't know where to start!"

Later that afternoon they were kicking a ball around in the back garden when Dad stopped for a moment to have a drink from his can of beer.

"You all right, Nath?" he asked. "You don't seem all that happy."

Of course, he was happy. He'd got the thing he'd wanted most in all the world. Dad was home. But he kept thinking about Ben. And Hayley. And Ben's mum.

And Dad guessed what was on his mind.

"It's Ben and his dad, isn't it?"

Nathan nodded. "It's like I grassed him up or something."

"You didn't grass him up. You did what you had to do. He'd killed people – he might have done it again. And he was ready to let me take the blame."

"I know," Nathan said. "But what about Ben? I mean, he can't help it if his dad's a monster."

Nathan was very tired that night. He was almost asleep when his dad came into his bedroom and sat on the end of the bed.

"I met all sorts in prison," his dad said. "Thieves, murderers – guys who'd done all kinds of dark stuff. And you know what? Not one of them was a monster. Messed up, mixed up, gone wrong – sometimes badly, badly wrong. But no monsters. All human beings. And they all had people who loved them."

There was a long silence. And it felt good to have his dad there.

"I think we ought to go round and see your mate tomorrow," his dad said. "Don't you?"

Nathan nodded.

Chapter 18
The Visit

There was a small group of people hanging around outside Ben's house. They booed and jeered and whistled and shouted swear words as Nathan and his dad walked up the path to the house.

When they got to the doorstep, Nathan felt very nervous. What was he going to say to Ben and his family?

He looked back at the group of people on the pavement. Their faces were filled with hatred and anger. A few weeks ago, people like that had stood outside his house, shouting the same things. But Ben had come to see him. Ben had stood by him. Well, he would stand by Ben.

He turned and rang the doorbell.

Barrington Stoke would like to thank all its readers for commenting on the manuscript before publication and in particular:

Jack Barnes

Anna Chorlton

Steven Cornish

Kelly Dawson

Laura Denness

Liz Devine

Mrs Entwistle

Jake Fenton

Ms Gillespie

Sam Gray

Kieron Ingram

Conor Keane

Scott Kyle

Matthew Lomax

Kyle McBain

Sophie McKie

Dana McKinney

Luke Millman

Ben Pople

Becky Powell

Lucy Price

Craig Reid

Matthew Shaw

Hannah Smith

Become a Consultant!

Would you like to give us feedback on our titles before they are published? Contact us at the email address below – we'd love to hear from you!

info@barringtonstoke.co.uk
www.barringtonstoke.co.uk